W9-AJN-804

HARRIS COUNTY PUBLIC LIBRARY

J Santop
Santopolo, Jill
Bling It On!

$5.99
ocn915045098
Aladdin paperback edition.

WITHDRAWN

Bling It On!

* .. * .. * * .. * *

Also by Jill Santopolo

Sparkle Spa

Book 7

Bling It On!

JILL SANTOPOLO

Aladdin

NEW YORK LONDON TORONTO SYDNEY NEW DELHI

If you purchased this book without a cover, you should be aware that this book is stolen property. It was reported as "unsold and destroyed" to the publisher, and neither the author nor the publisher has received any payment for this "stripped book."

This book is a work of fiction. Any references to historical events, real people, or real places are used fictitiously. Other names, characters, places, and events are products of the author's imagination, and any resemblance to actual events or places or persons, living or dead, is entirely coincidental.

ALADDIN

An imprint of Simon & Schuster Children's Publishing Division
1230 Avenue of the Americas, New York, NY 10020
This Aladdin paperback edition October 2015
Text copyright © 2015 by Simon & Schuster, Inc.
Cover illustrations copyright © 2015 by Cathi Mingus
Also available in an Aladdin hardcover edition.
All rights reserved, including the right of reproduction in whole or in part in any form.
ALADDIN is a trademark of Simon & Schuster, Inc., and related logo is
a registered trademark of Simon & Schuster, Inc.
For information about special discounts for bulk purchases, please contact
Simon & Schuster Special Sales at 1-866-506-1949 or business@simonandschuster.com.
The Simon & Schuster Speakers Bureau can bring authors to your live event. For more
information or to book an event, contact the Simon & Schuster Speakers Bureau
at 1-866-248-3049 or visit our website at www.simonspeakers.com.
Series design by Jeanine Henderson
Cover design by Laura Lyn DiSiena
The text of this book was set in Adobe Caslon.
Manufactured in the United States of America 0915 OFF
10 9 8 7 6 5 4 3 2 1
Library of Congress Control Number 2015908993
ISBN 978-1-4814-2391-5 (hc)
ISBN 978-1-4814-2390-8 (pbk)
ISBN 978-1-4814-2392-2 (eBook)

This one's in memory of my dad.

Gobs of glittery thanks to editrix Karen Nagel,
agent Miriam Altshuler, and writer buddies
Marianna Baer, Marie Rutkoski, and Eliot Schrefer.

Contents

Bling It On!

one

Blue Your Best

Aly Tanner sat in the back of the auditorium at Auden Elementary School in a chair the color of Blue Your Best nail polish. Looking at row after row of kids sitting in front of her reminded Aly of the ocean.

She was sitting between her best friends, Charlotte and Lily. Toward the middle of the room, Aly thought she could see the tip-top of her younger sister Brooke's head, tilted toward Brooke's best friend, Sophie Chu. Brooke was probably telling Sophie a story, because she was always telling stories, or asking questions, or wondering about things. Aly wondered if Brooke was the biggest chatterbox in the whole third grade. It was quite possible. She might even be the biggest chatterbox in all of Auden Elementary.

"May I have your attention! Boys and girls, your attention, please!" Principal Rogers was standing on the auditorium stage, with Assistant Principal Amari next to her. The whole room quieted down—Aly checked, and even Brooke was looking straight ahead.

"I'm here today to talk about Auden Elementary's Annual School Carnival!" Principal Rogers said.

All the kids cheered, including Aly. She loved the school carnival. There were a lot of booths. Last year Aly and Brooke had gotten their faces painted at the Face the Music booth and their hair spray-painted with purple stripes at Mane Event. And Aly had won two goldfish. She had carried them in their plastic bags around the carnival and named them Goldie and Lox. This year, Aly had no idea what she and her friends would do, but whatever it was, she knew it would be fun.

"Just like last year," Principal Rogers added, "the fifth and sixth graders are invited to submit proposals for booths. Assistant Principal Amari and I will choose twenty to be at the carnival."

Another cheer erupted from the room, but this time Aly didn't join them. She'd forgotten that fifth and sixth graders were the ones who ran the booths. She tucked her hair behind her ears, but as usual it didn't stay and flopped back in front of her eye. She'd have to decide between thinking up ideas with her friends and just going to the carnival like she did last year. Running a booth sounded like a lot of work, but it might be fun, too.

"Oh my gosh!" Charlotte whispered to Aly. "We could have a Sparkle Spa booth!"

Aly turned to look at her friend. "You think so?" she asked.

"It would be awesome," Lily whispered from Aly's other side. "We should *totally* do a Sparkle Spa booth."

Even though they were still in elementary school, Aly and her sister, Brooke, were in charge of the Sparkle Spa, a sparkly nail salon for kids that was in the back room of their mom's grown-up nail salon, True Colors. Charlotte and Lily, and Brooke's friend Sophie, sometimes worked there too. And once in a while Charlotte's twin brother, Caleb, helped out. Even though it was hard work running a salon, most of the time Aly thought it was pretty awesome, especially when kids at school told her how much they loved the way their nails looked at their dance recital or their aunt's wedding or their grandparents' anniversary dinner.

Aly figured that was how their mom felt, too, when she saw grown-ups with True Colors manicures and pedicures.

"Do you think anyone would come?" Aly asked. "I mean, it takes a long time to get your nails polished, compared to getting a flower painted on your face or throwing Ping-Pong balls into a cup of water to win a fish."

Charlotte tapped the little Sparkle Spa schedule book that was sticking out of Aly's jeans pocket. "You know how many customers come to the salon. Why wouldn't they come to a booth at the carnival?"

Charlotte seemed certain about this, but Aly wasn't so sure.

"Students," Principal Rogers continued, "this year we have a special addition to the carnival." She held up her hands so that people wouldn't start talking again and handed the microphone to Assistant Principal Amari.

"Hellooooo, boys and girls!" AP Amari said.

"Hellooooo, AP Amari!" everyone answered. AP Amari taught the school that call-and-response game at the beginning of each year. Aly liked the way he started an assembly.

"Who has heard of Water World Amusement Park?" he asked.

"Me!" almost everyone answered. Water World was a water park about half an hour's drive from Aly and Brooke's house. With fast slides that twisted and turned and the longest lazy river ever, it was a super-fun place. Last year Lily had her birthday party there.

"Who knows that all the money raised at our carnival is donated to the Auden Community Chest group, which helps food banks and other services for people who need help in our neighborhood?"

"Me!" fewer people said, mostly sixth graders.

"Well," said Mr. Amari, "Mr. Molina, the head of the Community Chest and *also* the owner of Water World told us that whatever we raise this year, he'll personally double that amount. More money for the Community Chest means we can help more people. So let's hear it for Mr. Molina!"

Everyone cheered.

Mr. Amari went on. "And because of Mr. Molina's offer, we've added a twist this year. Mr. Molina agreed to let us have a competition between the boys—led by me—and the girls—led by Principal Rogers. We'll see who can raise the most money. If the boys win, they get a day off from school to go to Water World!"

The boys stomped their feet. Aly did not. Neither did Lily or Charlotte.

"And if the girls raise the most money, *they* all

get a day off from school to go to Water World!"

This time Aly, Lily, and Charlotte cheered loudly. Lily stuck two fingers in her mouth and made a super-high-pitched whistle.

"Go, girls!" Charlotte shouted.

Her brother, Caleb, poked her in the shoulder. "Hey, stop that!" he said.

Then his friend Cameron leaned over. "You girls don't have a chance. Boys rule and are going to win."

Lily leaned across Aly. "Boys don't rule, they drool," she told him.

"No, Lily. *You'll* see. Boys will rule." Then Cameron added, "Let's make a side bet. If the boys win, you have to bring in a whole batch of those cookies you girls are always talking about."

Cookies? What cookies? Aly wondered.

"It's a bet, Cameron. You'll never taste Joan's awesome cookies," Charlotte answered this time.

Joan's cookies? What did Charlotte just do? How had Mom's best friend—and the girls' favorite manicurist—gotten in the middle of this? Now the girls had to win, because Aly didn't want to have to ask Joan to bake a whole batch of cookies for the boys!

Mr. Amari tapped the microphone. "Everyone has two days to come up with booth proposals. They are due in the main office by the time school starts on Thursday, and Principal Rogers and I will announce the booths at the end of the day."

Aly saw someone's hand waving in the air in the middle of the room. She realized it was Brooke's and groaned. What could Brooke possibly have to say? No one else in the auditorium had a question.

"Yes, Brooke Tanner?" AP Amari said.

Brooke stood up. "Do all the girls in the whole school get to go to Water World if the girls' booths make more money?"

"They do indeed," he answered.

"So how come only the fifth- and sixth-grade girls can run the booths? How come the third graders can't help?" Brooke tugged on her braid, which Aly knew she did when she was nervous or excited about something. Aly figured she was probably nervous now. But Aly understood why Brooke was asking that question: Brooke wanted a Sparkle Spa booth too, and knew it would never work without her and Sophie polishing.

"Good question, Brooke." Mr. Amari turned to Principal Rogers. "What do you think?" he asked her.

Principal Rogers took the microphone. "I think if our fifth and sixth graders want children from the younger grades to help, that's perfectly fine with me. If you need more workers, feel free to ask the kindergarteners through fourth graders. Good luck, everyone."

"Yes!" Brooke cheered, and sat down. Then she

popped up. "Thank you!" she squeaked, and sat down once more.

"Brooke and Sophie can help," Charlotte said, clapping. "That's perfect. Then our booth will have three manicurists, just like the salon."

Since Aly and Brooke were co-CEOs of the Sparkle Spa—initials that stood for chief executive officer and meant they were in charge of their business together—Aly figured Brooke would probably want to be co-CEO of the carnival booth, even if she wasn't a fifth or sixth grader. And Aly thought that was okay.

But would a Sparkle Spa booth actually make enough money for the carnival, especially since such a great prize—and Charlotte's cookie bet—was on the line? And then, just like that, Aly had a worse worry: What if their proposal for a Sparkle Spa booth *wasn't* chosen? What would they do then to win the prize?

two

Red-y, Set, Go

Aly and Brooke's mom had lots of rules for the Sparkle Spa:

1. It could be open three days a week (Tuesdays, Fridays, and Saturdays—unless a special event was scheduled).
2. They could offer four services to their customers (manicures, pedicures, hair braiding, bracelet making, but no makeup or tattoos).

And the most important one to Mom:

3. The girls had to finish homework
   before polishing nails.

Since it was Tuesday, the girls headed over to the
Sparkle Spa after school.

Tuesday was the sisters' favorite day at the salon.
That was when every single girl on the Auden Elementary soccer team—the Auden Angels—came to the
spa. Jenica Posner, the captain of the team and also the
coolest sixth grader, had really been the reason Aly and
Brooke started the Sparkle Spa in the first place.

A few months ago when all the True Colors manicurists were busy, Mom allowed Aly to give Jenica
a rainbow sparkle pedicure, and then Jenica played
really well in her soccer game. After that, the entire
soccer team wanted rainbow sparkle pedicures every

week—they were sure it gave them sparkle power. Their sparkle power took them all the way to the state finals, where they won!

Now the Angels were playing indoor soccer for the winter season and wanted to keep up their sparkle power, which meant pedicures every Tuesday.

"So," Jenica said as she climbed into one of the two pedicure chairs. "Are you going to have a Sparkle Spa booth at the carnival?"

Aly and Brooke had talked about it on the walk from school to the salon. Aly still wasn't convinced it was the best idea. And she hadn't mentioned a word about the Cameron and Charlotte Cookie Bet. Aly had made Charlotte promise not to say anything to anyone, just in case it somehow got back to her mother and Joan that they'd promised a batch of Joan's cookies without asking her first.

"Maybe," Brooke said. She turned on the faucet

in the pedicure basin, filling it with soapy water to soak Jenica's feet. "I think it's a good idea. Aly sort of does. But she's a little worried we won't make enough money at the carnival because of how long it takes us to do manicures."

"Right," Aly said. She was giving Anjuli Jones, the Angels' goalie, a pedicure. Anjuli always had her fingers polished as well as her toes. She switched up her colors each week, and this time she handed Aly a bottle of Red-y, Set, Go for her nails.

Brooke took a towel to dry off Jenica's feet. "Do you think any of the Angels would want to learn how to do manicures?" she asked. "If we had more people polishing, we could make more money at the booth."

Aly looked around at the Angels. Mia crinkled her nose. Bethany's face was scrunched up like she'd just sucked on an extra-sour piece of candy.

"Probably not," Jenica answered. "I think we should stick to what we're good at."

"Plus, we want to run a goalie booth," Mia added from the bracelet-making area. She was stringing blue and white beads onto a piece of wire. "People can pay a dollar to try and score a goal off Anjuli. If they do, we'll give them a prize."

"I don't think we'll need that many prizes," Bethany said, handing Mia a blue bead. "Hardly anyone ever scores off Anjuli."

Anjuli smiled as she dipped her toes into the basin in front of her. "Maybe I'll let some of the kindergarteners score on purpose, so they can get the prizes."

"And me," Brooke said. "You should let me score so *I* can get a prize."

Everyone in the salon laughed.

"That's a great idea for a booth," Lily said. She was standing at her favorite spot in the Sparkle Spa, between the teal strawberry-shaped donation jar and the polish wall. She liked to help people pick out colors if they weren't sure which ones they wanted. And when they were done, she reminded customers to make a donation before they left.

Another one of Mom's rules was that the girls couldn't charge for their services, but they could ask for donations. The Sparkle Spa donated the money they got to whatever local charity they agreed could use the help.

"Hey, everyone, don't forget your donations on the way out!" Lily said, pointing to the sparkly teal strawberry.

"Have you ever given the Sparkle Spa donations to the Community Chest?" Jenica asked.

Aly hadn't thought about that, but it wasn't a bad idea. She gave Brooke a Secret Sister Eye Message: *What do you think?*

Brooke nodded.

"That's a great thought," Aly said. "I wonder . . ." She paused. "I wonder if we can have it count toward the girls' money at the carnival?"

Charlotte was standing at the appointment wall, where the Sparkle Spa schedule was taped up. "Probably not," she said. "The rules were about who raises the most money at the carnival, not just who donates the most."

"That's a good point," Brooke said. "Maybe we can ask some younger kids if they want to learn how to give manicures. Principal Rogers said they're allowed to help at the booth."

Aly shuddered at the thought of trying to teach kindergarteners how to polish nails. But then again, she'd first learned in kindergarten. "Maybe," she said.

"Maybe what?"

Aly turned around as her mom walked into the

Sparkle Spa, went over to the mini-fridge, and took out a bottle of water.

"Maybe we'll have a Sparkle Spa booth at the school carnival and train other kids to do manicures," Brooke told her. "Because we want the girls to win so we can go to Water World for free."

Mom took a sip of water. "It sounds like there's a lot more to this story that I need to hear later."

"There is, Mrs. Tanner," Lily said.

"We can talk at dinner," Mom said to Aly and Brooke.

Aly wondered what her mom would think about training kindergarteners. Since Mom was the CEO of True Colors, Aly and Brooke asked her their business questions all the time, and she almost always knew the right answers.

Mom left the salon, and Aly returned to Anjuli's toes.

The afternoon went quickly, especially after Sophie arrived and started to help. She was the Sparkle Spa's third manicurist but had to come late that day.

"Sorry," she said. "Dentist."

The Angels nodded in sympathy.

Once the Auden Angels had their toes done and Lily and Charlotte and Sophie had gone home, Aly and Brooke were alone in the Sparkle Spa, straightening up. Brooke was reorganizing the bottles on the polish wall, arranging them in color order. Aly was putting all the trash in one big bag so they could take it to the Dumpster outside.

All of a sudden, Brooke stopped, a bottle of Starlight Starbright in her hand. "I've got it!" she yelped. "We can add a fast treatment to the Sparkle Spa booth!"

Aly tied the trash bag. "Fast treatment?"

Brooke pushed her glasses up on her nose. "We shouldn't *just* do manicures. You and Charlotte are both really good at hair braiding, and it's really quick to do. We can do 'slow' manicures and 'fast' hair braiding, and then we'll make a lot more money."

Aly thought it through. "Yes!" she said to Brooke. "That's perfect!"

Then she thought for a second more. "What if you and Sophie braided too, and we just had a *braiding* booth?"

Brooke tugged on her own braid—a fishbone one that Aly had done that morning—and said, "Well, I think our customers are expecting a Sparkle Spa manicure booth. After the assembly, everyone was talking about it—so I think we have to have one. Right?"

"I guess so," Aly said. "And maybe Principal Rogers is more likely to pick our idea if we have both.

I'll call Lily and Charlotte tonight, and we can all work on the application tomorrow after school."

"Yesss!" Brooke said. "I can't wait to tell Sophie."

Aly found herself smiling as she went to toss the trash bag into the Dumpster. Brooke always came up with the best ideas. For the first time since Lily suggested the booth, Aly felt like they had a really good shot at making money for the girls' team. Hopefully, Principal Rogers would feel the same way!

three
Write Bright

The next day at lunch, Aly, Lily and Charlotte were hanging out on the monkey bars. Lily was dangling from the first bar, trying to do a pull-up. But her left arm was a little bit stronger than her right, so she could only do it partway. She jumped down to the ground and Charlotte climbed up. Charlotte couldn't do a pull-up at all, but she did have a good view of the rest of the playground.

"Suzy Davis Alert!" Charlotte blurted, and jumped down. "She's on her way over."

About thirty seconds later, Suzy Davis showed up. Lately, it seemed that Aly and her friends couldn't escape Suzy. She *always* showed up at recess when they were together: They couldn't be at the monkey bars or the tire swing or the hopscotch court without Suzy butting in.

Aly and Suzy Davis used to not like each other at all. But a few weeks ago, for School Picture Day, Suzy had started her own business, which she called Suzy's Spectacular Makeup. She put fairy dust and shimmer lip gloss on anyone who was willing to pay a dollar. The business had almost been a disaster until Aly, Lily, and Charlotte helped her out. After that, Suzy wasn't as mean to Aly as she used to be, and Aly liked Suzy a little bit more, but they still were definitely not friends.

"So are you going to have a Sparkle Spa booth for the carnival?" Suzy asked.

"That's our plan," Aly said. "But we still have to write our proposal."

"I finished my proposal already," Suzy said, leaning against the metal pole that held up the monkey bars. "It's going to be Suzy's Spectacular Makeup, just like on Picture Day, but even better because now I also have perfume. Everyone will get fairy dust and shimmer lip gloss and a spritz of perfume. It'll be the best booth at the whole carnival. The girls' side will win because of me."

"That sounds great," Aly said. "Are you going to ask younger kids to work the booth with you?"

"Good question," Lily said as she climbed back up onto the first monkey bar. "Because last time we had to help you, remember? You couldn't do it fast enough all by yourself."

"Whatever," Suzy said, pushing herself off the pole. "I bet Principal Rogers isn't going to pick your booth anyway, even if you have a million people working there. No one wants to sit for a manicure in the middle of a carnival."

She started walking away, and Charlotte yelled after her. "We're doing hair braiding, too!"

Lily finally pulled herself up and got her chin up over the bar. "I did it!" she said, and then jumped off the bar.

"Nice!" Charlotte said.

Aly gave Lily a hug. She'd been trying to do a chin-up on the monkey bars for at least a month now. But even while she was hugging Lily, Aly was worrying about what Suzy Davis had said. Even with the braiding, would people want to come to their booth?

That afternoon, Aly, Brooke, Charlotte, and Sophie—Lily had basketball practice—headed to the Sparkle Spa to work on the carnival application.

As the girls walked over, Aly read the questions out loud.

"Name of Booth," she said.

"That one's easy peasy," Brooke answered. "The Sparkle Spa Booth."

"Hmm," Charlotte said. "Should it be something catchier than that? The Sparkle Spa Booth doesn't sound all that . . . exciting."

Aly agreed with Charlotte, but she also thought Brooke's name made a lot of sense. They wanted people to know what they were getting, and it seemed like everyone at school knew about the Sparkle Spa.

"*I* think it sounds exciting," said Brooke. "Right, Sophie?" She turned to look at Sophie.

"Well," said Sophie. "I'm not sure. . . ."

Sophie was always honest and never ever wanted to be mean, so if she wasn't agreeing with Brooke,

Aly knew the name needed some help. But she also knew that the words "Sparkle Spa" should stay. She made a quick list inside her head. She imagined it looking like this:

Other Words to Use Instead of Booth
Spot
Space
Surprises
Celebration

"Celebration!" Aly said out loud. "What about calling the booth A Sparkle Spa Celebration? And we could decorate it like it was a party."

"Love it, Aly!" Brooke said.

"I like it too," said Sophie as she pushed open the door to True Colors.

"Me three," said Charlotte, following Sophie inside.

"Definitely exciting. And now we have a decoration theme."

Aly walked in after Charlotte, and Brooke came in last. Everyone in the salon—all the manicurists and customers—turned to say hello, and Aly and Brooke's mom said, "Hi, girls. Snacks in the back, as usual."

"And some extra cookies," Joan added. Even though she was COO of the salon, Joan still gave manicures, so she was sitting at manicure station number seven, polishing Mrs. Franklin's nails. Besides being an awesome manicurist, Joan was an amazing baker. She brought the girls cookies all the time. That's why the cookie bet—which Aly didn't want to think about just then—had happened.

"Thanks, Joan," Aly said, feeling guilty about the mention of cookies—just as Brooke said, "Mom! Guess what! Aly came up with the best theme for our booth at the carnival. It's going to be a celebration party theme."

"That sounds great," Mom said. She was putting a coat of clear polish on Mrs. Howard's nails, which were painted White Bright, a new color that shimmered like opals. It was Aly's favorite of that week's polish shipment. "I can't wait to hear about it later."

The girls went to the Sparkle Spa and sprawled across the floor, eating cheese and crackers and cookies and finishing their homework before Aly pulled out the application form. She started filling it in with the decisions the girls had made on the walk over:

Name of Booth: A Sparkle Spa Celebration

Description of Booth: At our booth, people will be able to get their nails polished with sparkly

colors and will also be able to
get their hair braided in many
different styles.

What You Will Charge:

"Guys?" she asked. "How much should we charge for manicures and braids?"

"I wish Lily were here!" said Charlotte. Lily was technically the Sparkle Spa's CFO, which stood for chief financial officer. She was in charge of counting the money, making sure they had enough to pay Mom for their supplies and seeing how much was left over for donations.

"Last time we ran an event where we were raising money, we charged five dollars for a manicure," Sophie said. "Maybe we could do that again."

Brooke said, "How about one dollar for a braid? Or maybe two dollars?"

"Let's do two dollars," Aly said. "So that we make more money."

Brooke nodded. Aly wrote that down.

The next question was about what supplies they'd need and the budget, or how much the supplies would cost. Aly wrote: "free." The girls decided the Sparkle Spa would donate nail polish and glittery hair elastics, plus they had a bag of extra balloons and party streamers from a spa party they'd had for the Auden Angels.

Brooke looked over Aly's shoulder and read the application. "Should we include the party theme somewhere?" she asked.

Aly shrugged. She wasn't sure if it would make a difference, but she wrote it in the description section, adding the words "party-themed" in between "our" and "booth."

Charlotte inspected the application. So did Sophie.

"I think this looks great," Charlotte said.

Sophie agreed.

"Okay, just one last thing, then," Aly said, taking out her pen. She wrote her name, Charlotte's, and Lily's at the bottom of the form. Then she put Brooke's and Sophie's names as helpers. "All done!" she said.

And then Lily burst into the Sparkle Spa. Her hair was sweaty from basketball and plastered to the side of her face.

"This is an emergency!" she said. "We have to do something more with the Sparkle Spa booth or we'll never be chosen. Charlotte, your brother was talking with Garrett at basketball and they're getting cool tattoos for people at their booth. Temporary tattoos! Everybody is going to want one of those. Boys *and* girls. And that means more dollars for them! Plus, it only takes like twenty seconds to put on a temporary tattoo!"

"What do you mean more money because of boys and girls?" Brooke asked.

But Aly understood already. "She means," Aly told her sister, "that if there are one hundred kids at the carnival, and fifty are boys and fifty are girls, we could *maybe* get all the girls and a small number of boys to come to our booth. But the boys' booth could attract all the girls *and* all the boys, because everyone can get a tattoo. But not everyone has hair long enough for braids or likes sparkly nail polish. Mostly just girls do."

"Oh," said Brooke. Then, "Oh," again.

"Like I said, we need to think of something else," Lily said, plopping down onto one of the floor pillows in the nail-drying area.

Aly's thoughts raced. They could sell beaded bracelets or necklaces. But those took a lot of work to make, plus bracelet making wasn't all that exciting for a carnival booth.

"What if we bring Sparkly, and people can pay to pet him?" Brooke suggested.

Aly looked at Sparkly, the girls' tiny dog, who was asleep in his corner. Would Sparkly really like being part of a booth? And Aly doubted Principal Rogers would even allow dogs at the carnival.

"What about a photo booth, like the one for the soccer party?" Sophie asked.

Brooke nodded, changing idea directions. "I could do really cool backgrounds. Ones that boys would like, no problem."

Aly tapped her pen against the floor. "We do have the Polaroid camera," she said. "We'd just have to buy film."

"Film is a little expensive," Lily said, sitting down next to Aly. She looked over at the application. "Look," she said. "There's a space for a budget from the school. We won't have to take too much out of our donation jar. If we want to take a hundred pictures, the budget would be a hundred dollars for film. That doesn't seem like too much, does it?"

Aly liked this idea. Hopefully, the school would be willing to pay, or at least chip in some money.

"Do we need more pictures, though?" Charlotte asked. "Our school has four hundred and six kids in it."

"And don't forget about little brothers and sisters," said Sophie.

"Well," said Aly, "not everyone's going to want a picture. And more than one person can be in a picture at a time. So let's say two hundred pictures. That's two hundred dollars. I hope that's okay for the school. And we can charge two dollars per photo."

Aly looked around. Everyone was nodding. "Brooke?" she asked. Since Brooke was the co-CEO, she had to agree with every Sparkle Spa decision one hundred percent.

"Let's do it!" Brooke said.

Aly added the information to the application. "Okay," she said. "I'll hand it in first thing tomorrow."

"Let's keep our shoelaces crossed all day," Brooke said. "For luck."

Sophie looked down at her feet. "My shoelaces are *always* crossed."

"That must be why you're so lucky," Brooke laughed.

Aly smiled at her sister. But she thought about extra-crossing her shoelaces tomorrow just in case.

four

Red It Be

Aly and Brooke raced to get ready for school the next morning to make sure they made the application deadline. Aly stared at her polka-dot watch while Mom was stopped at a red light.

"We only have seven minutes, Mom!" Aly said.

"We're only two minutes away from school," Mom answered. "You'll have more than enough time."

Aly put her backpack on while she was still in the car, and Brooke did the same. They leaned forward like turtles with their hands on their seat belts, ready to unhook them as soon as they reached the car pool drop-off area.

"Love you, Mom! See you later!" Aly said when Mom stopped the car.

Once the sisters were out of the car, they ran, in their crisscross-laced sneakers, inside the front door and straight to a table outside the main office. They dropped the form into a box marked AUDEN CARNIVAL APPLICATIONS. Principal Rogers was standing next to the box.

"Good luck, girls," she said.

Aly smiled at her. Brooke said, "I really, really hope you pick our booth. It's fun and everyone will love it a lot. We'll make so much money for the Community Chest and then the girls will win a free water park day."

Principal Rogers grinned.

As Aly and Brooke headed to their classes, they

had to wade through groups of students hurrying down the hall to drop off their applications.

That whole day, Aly had a hard time concentrating. All she could think about was the announcement that afternoon, and the booths everyone was talking about. She even made lists.

<u>Booth Ideas I Don't Like</u>

1. Theo Anderson's Lick a Lizard idea. He wants people to pay $1 to lick his pet lizard. No way would Principal Rogers agree to that.

2. Maddy Leder's Counting Bubbles. How could anyone actually count them once they sailed away?

3. Bob Stillman's Shake a Stick. It sounds super boring.

Booth Ideas I Like

1. Oliver Shin's Figure It Out!
   You stick your hand into a box
   and touch something and guess
   what it is, and if you get all
   the identifications right, you
   win a prize. Cool.
2. The Auden Angels' Soccer
   Score. Angels stuff is
   always cool.
3. Suzy's Spectacular Makeup.
   Have to admit, people will go.
4. Peter's Penny Guess. How
   many pennies will be in that
   giant jar?
5. Ivy and Paige's Fortune-Teller.
   I wonder if their fortunes will
   come true?

But then Aly heard that a sixth grader named Aubrey—whose nails Aly had painted Red It Be the week before—was going to run a photo booth with her friends Maisie and Jade. They called it Be a Super-Model and planned to have different-color backgrounds, along with costume pieces and props like hats and boas and masks and magic wands. Instead of a Polaroid camera, they were going to borrow Aubrey's dad's digital camera and printer, so they could make as many copies of each picture as they'd like.

Aly's stomach flip-flopped when she heard that. That sounded like a better photo booth than theirs. And if Principal Rogers picked Be a Super-Model, did it mean she wouldn't pick the Sparkle Spa booth? Aly looked down at her crossed shoelaces and hoped they'd do their magic.

Right before the end of the day, Aly was sitting at her desk finishing up Sustained Silent Reading. Her

SSR book was *Here's to You, Rachel Robinson*, by an author named Judy Blume. Aly really liked this book and usually had no problem paying attention to the story, but today she could barely focus on Rachel.

She jumped when the PA system beeped. She stopped reading and looked up at the speaker on the wall.

"Hello, students," Principal Rogers said.

"Helloooo, Auden Elementary!" AP Amari added.

Aly smiled as her whole class answered, "Helloooo, AP Amari!" even though he couldn't hear them. AP Amari could make any announcement sound fun, even if it was one that made her worried.

"We've chosen the carnival booths," Principal Rogers began. "This was a very tough decision, and you all came up with wonderful ideas. AP Amari is going to list the ten boys' booths first, and then I'm going to list the ten girls' booths. Auden Elementary is filled with smart, talented, creative students, and I'm honored to be your principal. Now, AP Amari, take it away!"

"Okay, boys' team, here we go!" AP Amari bellowed. "At the carnival we're going to have: Oliver Shin's Figure It Out!, the sixth-grade boys' basketball team's Can You Dribble It?, Daniel Martinez and Bennett Johnson's Win a Fish!—I always love a good fish booth, don't you?"

"Yes!" a few kids in Aly's class responded, including Daniel and Bennett, who had huge smiles on their faces. Aly would've laughed if she hadn't been so nervous.

AP Amari continued. "Then we have Caleb Cane, Garrett Brower, and Cameron Castelli's Tattoo You booth."

A huge cheer erupted from where Caleb, Garrett, and Cameron sat. Cameron looked over at Charlotte and rubbed his stomach, pretending he had just eaten a cookie. Charlotte ignored him.

And then Suzy Davis shushed the boys. "I want to hear!" she said.

"For our fifth booth, we have Lucas Grant and Lee Goldenberg's Name That Tune," AP Amari said, "then Sebastian Gray's Wheel of Chance, the boys of the checkers club's King Me, Simon Lebret's Find the Rock Under the Cups, Ian Sachs and Chris Gomez's Sports Trivia, and last, but certainly not least, Ryan Fishman's Roll a Hole in One. Congratulations, boys."

"Oh, man!" Theo Anderson said when AP Amari stopped talking. "I can't believe my Lick a Lizard booth didn't get chosen."

In the meantime, Caleb, Garrett, and Cameron were high-fiving again, and so were Daniel and Bennett. The rest of the boys who had won were in different classes. Most of them were sixth graders, Aly noticed. She hoped that didn't mean sixth graders got priority.

"Now," Principal Rogers said, "I'm happy to announce that we have ten wonderful booths from the girls this year."

Aly held her breath.

"First we have the Auden Angels' Soccer Score, then Daisy Quinn and Uma Prasad's Paint Your Face, Talia Lieber's Create a Cookie, Maria Sanchez and Sara Robinson's Marry Me, Samara Amin's Wheel of Fortune, the Carson triplets' Famous Facts, Carina Chang and Daniella Snow's Soda Straw Spin Art, Kerry McCarthy's Balloon Darts, and Aubrey Adair, Maisie Wallis, and Jade Marino's Be a Super-Model."

Aly was counting. That was nine. She let out her breath. Why had Principal Rogers stopped talking? What was number ten?

"For our final booth," Principal Rogers said, "we're doing something unusual. We're asking the students to make a small tweak to their proposal. When this announcement is over, will Aly Tanner, Charlotte Cane, and Lily Myers please come to the main office? Our final booth is going to be A Sparkle Spa Celebration. Congratulations, girls!"

The end-of-the-day bell rang, and everyone in Aly's class got up to grab their backpacks off the hooks in the back of the room. Instead of grabbing her backpack, Aly ran to Charlotte's desk. Lily was there too.

"What do you think Principal Rogers wants from us?" Lily asked, just as Charlotte said, "Our booth got chosen!"

Aly looked at Charlotte first. "I know!"

Then she turned to Lily. "I don't know!"

Charlotte and Lily both laughed, but Aly didn't.

She didn't like it when she couldn't figure out why someone wanted to talk to her about something.

"Come in, girls, come in," Principal Rogers said when the girls reached her office.

Aly had never been in the principal's office before. She couldn't help looking around. There was an orange couch the exact color of Teeny Tangeriney polish, a huge wood desk, four really tall bookcases filled with books and picture frames and a tennis racket, and a red, orange, and yellow striped rug on the floor.

"I like the idea of your booth, girls," Principal Rogers said, "and am thrilled to have you include your braiding and nail polishing at the carnival. I think you'll raise a lot of money for the girls' team. *But* I'm afraid you're not going to be able to have a photo booth. The budget is too high, and Aubrey, Maisie, and Jade's Super-Model booth is very similar, but much less expensive."

Aly swallowed. "But that was how we were going to make extra money and maybe get the boys as customers too." *And not have to ask Joan to bake,* Aly thought.

Lily and Charlotte nodded.

Principal Rogers thought for moment. "Well, I wouldn't worry too much about appealing to the boys. I think you'll get enough customers at your booth to keep you busy for the whole carnival. However, if you'd like to think of an additional idea, that would be fine. It just can't be a duplicate concept or theme."

"Okay," Aly answered. "Thanks, Principal Rogers."

The girls shuffled out of the office and down the hall. Aly was happy and relieved about being chosen, but what would they come up with? She really didn't think manicures and braiding would be enough on their own. Especially since the boys were doing tattoos. *Maybe we should have included Sparkly,* Aly sighed to herself, even though the idea wasn't great.

five

Deep Blue Sea

The next day at lunch, Aly was feeling mopey. She and Brooke had talked the night before and couldn't come up with one good idea to add to the Sparkle Spa Celebration booth. She was also feeling a bit guilty over not telling Brooke about the cookie bet. Or Mom. Or Joan. Or anyone.

"Brooke thinks we should just leave it with manicures and braiding and nothing else," Aly told Charlotte and Lily as she took a bite of her cheese sandwich. Even her lunch seemed sad today. A cheese sandwich, an apple, water, and a bag of pretzels. Sad sad sad.

"I really think we should add something else," Charlotte said, biting into a donut. Aly was pretty sure her own mother would not consider a donut with frosting and sprinkles and something gooey inside appropriate lunch food.

"But what?" Aly answered. She knew Charlotte was trying to help with the bet too. "With everything Brooke and I thought of, either another booth is doing it, or it's too expensive, or too hard to pull off."

"Well, what was on your list?" Lily asked. "Maybe we'll come up with something new."

Aly pulled the Sparkle Spa schedule notebook out of her pocket and turned to the inside cover, where she had written the list. She handed it to Lily.

Lily read, then sighed. "You're right," she said. "This has pretty much everything."

"Let me see." Charlotte looked over Lily's shoulder. Aly could see Charlotte's lips moving as she read everything from glitter tattoos (the boys were doing tattoos, so that was out), to face paint (Daisy and Uma were doing that one), to make your own bracelets (too expensive), to make a music video (too expensive *and* too hard to pull off), to spin art (ditto—and also too similar to Carina and Daniella's booth).

Aly was taking another bite of her sandwich when someone asked, "Is anyone sitting here?"

The someone asking was Suzy Davis. And Suzy Davis rarely asked anything. If there was space at a table, Suzy usually just sat in it, even if someone else was trying to save it for a friend.

"Um, no," Aly said. "You can sit there if you want."

"Thanks," Suzy said, and she sat down. She didn't say one mean word or make fun of the Sparkle Spa or anything. Aly was almost worried about her.

"Are you okay, Suzy?" Aly asked.

"What do *you* think?" Suzy asked. She looked down at her yogurt instead of at Aly.

"You're upset about not being chosen for the carnival?" Aly asked it like a question, just in case she was wrong.

"You must be a genius for figuring that out," Suzy said. But there wasn't as much energy in her insult as usual.

"I'm sorry your booth wasn't picked," Aly said. "It was a good idea."

"Then maybe you're not a genius after all," Suzy said, "because Principal Rogers didn't think it was."

"If it makes you feel any better, she made us take the photo booth off our Sparkle Spa Celebration booth."

Suzy shrugged. "Aubrey's is a better photo booth anyway."

Aly took a sip of water. "I know. But I'm still bummed about it."

Suzy nodded.

Aly didn't say anything to her after that, and Suzy didn't say anything to Aly. But Aly somehow felt more connected to Suzy than she ever had before.

After school that day, the Sparkle Spa team met at Charlotte's house, making plans and lists for their booth. They talked about which polish colors to bring from the salon, how many glittery elastics they'd need to buy for braids, and booth theme decorations.

"Can we afford more balloons?" Brooke asked. "We only have seven left over in the closet, and I don't think that's enough."

Lily pulled Charlotte's mom's laptop closer to her and checked on the prices for balloons. "Balloons are really cheap," she said. "I think we can get those, no problem."

Brooke wasn't finished. "We need big brown paper, too. I already have markers, so we won't need any of those."

Gurgle. Gurgle.

Brooke started giggling. "What was *that*?" she asked.

"My stomach," Charlotte laughed. "Does anyone want grapes? I'm starving."

"We heard," Lily said.

Charlotte headed into the kitchen. But a minute later she came running back out without any grapes.

"Guys!" she said. "The boys are in the kitchen. They just said they're doing something *extra*-special for their booth that's going to make them win for sure, because every single person is going to want one. But they won't tell me what it is!"

Aly could feel the girls' trip to Water World slipping away. And the cookies.

"How could the boys possibly make tattoos more special?" Lily wondered. "I know what we have to do," she said. "Charlotte, you need to be a spy."

"A spy?" Sophie asked. "Like, sneak up on the boys and listen to what they're saying?"

"Exactly," said Lily. "Listen with your ear to the door. And since it's your house, you can go anywhere you want."

Charlotte smiled. "Well, it's a little sneaky, but I like this plan. Aly, do you want to spy with me? Four ears are better than two."

Aly thought eavesdropping on people was probably not the nicest thing to do, but she was desperate to find out the boys' secret plan, and she knew Charlotte was too. "Okay," she said. "I'll do it."

The girls decided they needed an alibi, in case the

boys saw them. They went to the kitchen and grabbed a bunch of grapes. Then they tiptoed past the closed door of Caleb's room.

"I'm going to drop a grape," Charlotte whispered. "Then we'll both bend down to pick it up, and listen at the crack in the bottom of the door. If anyone comes by, like my mom, or if one of the boys opens Caleb's door, we'll have an excuse."

"Maybe you should drop two grapes," Aly suggested. "So we each have one to pick up."

"Good plan," Charlotte agreed. She dropped the grapes on the floor, and she and Aly crouched down quietly. Aly stared at the Deep Blue Sea carpeting and listened as hard as she could. Once she strained her ears, she could hear Caleb's, Garrett's, and Cameron's voices. They had Caleb and Charlotte's dad's iPad and were choosing tattoos to order from an online store.

"Let's get some sports ones," Cameron said.

"Okay," Caleb said. "How about five baseball, five soccer, five basketball, and five football?"

"We should order some extra soccer balls, in case the Angels want some," Garrett said. "And some stars and hearts and other things that girls seem to like."

Aly smiled. It was nice that Garrett was making sure there were soccer balls for the Angels—and she knew some girls who came to the Sparkle Spa who would love star and heart tattoos. But they still hadn't heard anything that sounded top secret.

"We can get *special* star ones," Caleb said.

Aly looked at Charlotte. *Aha*—this might be it. Aly held her breath.

"Oh yeah?" Cameron said. "They have glow-in-the-dark stars? That's great, then. We should order double the amount."

Aly opened her eyes wide. Glow-in-the-dark tattoos. That must be the secret. She grabbed the grape closest to her off the floor, Charlotte grabbed the other one, and they raced back to tell the rest of the girls.

But even though they'd figured out the secret, Aly thought, they couldn't do anything about it.

Six

Cheer Up, Buttercup

"A re you ready *yet*?" Brooke shouted up the stairs. Aly and Brooke were in the kitchen, but their parents were still upstairs.

While they waited for their parents to drive them to the carnival, Aly was busy double-checking the wheelie suitcase that was filled with:

> balloons
> streamers
> Scotch tape

polishing tools like emery boards
and hand cream
exactly 498 glittery hair elastics

Aly pulled out the list of nail polish colors they had packed the night before:

Carnival Polishes
Cherry on Top (red)
Orange You Happy (orange)
Cheer Up, Buttercup (yellow)
Oscar the Green (green)
Deep Blue Sea (blue)
We the Purple (purple)
Cotton Candyland (pink)
Silver Celebration (silver)
Golden Oldies (gold)
Witches' Brew (black)

They were all there, two bottles of each.

"Mom and Dad, I said, are you ready yet?" Brooke called up the stairs, louder this time.

Still no one answered, so Brooke went marching up the steps.

Aly checked on the beautiful and sparkly poster Brooke had made, which was carefully rolled up so it wouldn't crease.

Then Brooke came back downstairs, with Mom and Dad following. "They're finally ready," she announced.

"We are," Dad said, laughing. "Are you girls ready for your big day?"

"It's not *such* a big day, Dad," Brooke said. "It's not like the day we opened the Sparkle Spa."

"Still, it's not every day you run a booth at a carnival," he answered.

Aly smiled. "You're right, Dad," she said, and

handed Brooke the poster to carry outside. "I'm so glad it's happening when you're home."

Aly and Brooke's dad traveled all the time—usually from Mondays until Fridays—but sometimes he worked on Saturdays and Sundays too. Aly felt lucky he was home this weekend so he could see the booth.

The Tanners piled into the car.

"Are you sure you have everything?" Mom asked.

Aly nodded. "I double-checked twice," she said.

"Does that mean you checked *four* times?" Brooke asked.

Aly counted. "Three," she said. "I checked once, then double-checked, then double-checked again."

"I think you triple-checked," Brooke said.

The whole family laughed.

Once they got to Auden Elementary, the girls' carnival team had a meeting with Principal Rogers.

The boys were on the other side of the field, meeting with AP Amari.

Principal Rogers wore the same outfit she wore each year for the carnival: Auden's school colors, a purple shirt and gold pants, and purple sneakers with gold soles. She raised her voice above the chattering girls. "Good morning, girls. We've got a busy day today, so please listen carefully. All of the girls' booths will be on the right side of the field, and all of the boys' booths will be on the left. You'll have thirty minutes for setup. The carnival begins at ten o'clock and will end at three o'clock."

Principal Rogers continued, "Do you see those thermometers over there?"

Aly saw a big painted thermometer with dollar signs on it. One was painted purple and the other was painted gold.

"Ours is the gold one, girls," Principal Rogers said.

"Every half hour, please have someone from your booth bring me whatever money you've made that last half hour. I will tally it on our thermometer. I'm so proud of your ideas this year. I truly believe you can win it."

Aly and Charlotte exchanged looks and crossed their fingers.

Principal Rogers handed out the carnival maps. When Brooke looked at the paper, she squealed, "We're next to cotton candy!"

Aly nodded. "I think that's a great spot. Everyone loves cotton candy. I bet we'll get a lot of traffic."

"Kids might even walk over for a braid while they're still eating cotton candy," Lily said.

As the Sparkle Spa team was heading to their spot, Principal Rogers asked, "What did you girls decide to add instead of the photo booth?"

Aly looked at Brooke. "Actually," she said, "we couldn't think of anything."

"That's too bad," their principal said. "But if you happen to think of anything else during the day, please let me know and I'll give you permission."

Once the girls reached their spot, they quickly taped up their sign, blew up balloons, and decorated with streamers for the party theme. Sophie and Brooke set up two manicure stations, and Charlotte and Aly set up two braiding stations.

"If more people want manicures than braiding, I'll go back and forth," Aly said, reminding everyone of the plan.

"Right," Brooke said.

Lily had brought the teal strawberry donation jar from the Sparkle Spa and was holding it carefully. "I'll collect all the money and bring it to Principal Rogers every half hour."

At 10:00 a.m. sharp, AP Amari blew a whistle into a bullhorn. The gates opened and kids and parents came rushing onto the school field.

Boys and girls rushed over to the carnival booths—Wheel of Chance, Soccer Score, and Win a Fish. Luckily, a few walked straight toward the Sparkle Spa booth, and soon Sophie and Brooke were polishing and Charlotte and Aly were braiding as fast as they could.

"Can I have a Dutch braid?" a fourth grader named Eliza asked.

Aly nodded. "No problem. Please give Lily two dollars, and come sit down."

As Aly was finishing Eliza's braid, Clementine, a third grader in Brooke's class, came over. "Can you give me two braids, one on each side?" she asked.

"Absolutely," Aly told her.

Clementine handed two dollars to Lily and waited patiently until Aly snapped the rubber band around the bottom of Eliza's braid.

As Clementine sat down, Aly looked over at Brooke and Sophie. "How's it going with the manicures?" she shouted to them. There were so many people at the carnival, she practically had to scream to be heard.

"We're fine," Brooke and Sophie both answered.

Mom and Dad came by, eating cotton candy. Mr. Tanner had won a box of golf balls from the Sports Trivia booth.

"The Sports Trivia booth?" Brooke asked. She was busy polishing the nails of Tuesday Martin, another third grader. "That's a *boy* booth! You're raising money for the boys, Dad! That's the wrong side! Quick—go to another girl booth."

"What's going on?" the girls' dad asked their mom.

"It's a competition," Mom said. "Remember, the girls told you last night at dinner? If the girls raise more money than the boys, they get to go to Water World for free. If not, the boys do."

"That's right," Dad said. "Now I remember. Sorry, Brookie. How about if I go . . . decorate a cookie over at that booth?"

Aly looked over at Talia Lieber's booth. Cookies in fun shapes like robots, dogs, and stars looked like they might be as tasty as Joan's. Aly hadn't forgotten for one second about Cameron and Charlotte's bet. She sure hoped carnival-goers were visiting more of the girls' booths than the boys' booths.

"Good plan, Dad," she said. "Maybe you and Mom should decorate two . . . and share with us."

"Actually," Mom said, "I think we'll decorate one for each of your team. Five cookies, coming up. Let's go, Mark."

Lily ran the Sparkle Spa Celebration money to Principal Rogers while Aly gave a French braid to

Jayden Smith and Sophie polished Marla Goodman's nails with Orange You Happy.

Brooke had just finished a Golden Oldies manicure when AP Amari blew his whistle. He was also dressed in purple and gold from head to toe, and was standing next to the thermometers with a can of red paint.

"I have an announcement to make!" he bellowed. "Right now the boys have made three hundred twenty-four dollars." Yelps and cheers of "Boys rule!" were heard from the boys' side of the field.

The assistant principal went on. "And the girls have made three hundred two dollars. Good work, everyone! I'll be painting the money onto the thermometers so everyone can see how they're doing!"

Brooke groaned. "The boys are winning. I wish I could polish faster. And that Dad didn't give that dumb Sports Trivia booth a dollar."

Charlotte groaned too. "*I* wish we could come up with one more thing for our booth, like Principal Rogers said. There are two problems, though. One, we can't think of anything. And two, we'd need someone else to do it, because we're all so busy."

Jayden jumped off the chair, and Hannah and Parker Stevens, twins in Mrs. Wexler's fourth-grade class, asked about braids.

Aly had started braiding Parker's hair in a fishbone when she saw Suzy Davis walk by with her sister and her dad. And all of a sudden, Aly had a fantastic idea.

Seven
Cherry on Top

Aly quickly finished Parker's braids and walked to the other side of the booth, where Brooke was polishing Zorah's pinkie with Cherry on Top.

"Brooke," Aly said, "I need to talk to you over here."

"I'm in the middle of a manicure," Brooke said.

"I know," Aly said. "But this is very important. I have an idea. For something to add to our booth."

"Okay, okay, I'm coming," Brooke said. She turned to Zorah. "I'm really sorry, but I'll be back in two seconds. Well, maybe ten seconds. But as fast as I can. I promise."

"Suzy Davis is the answer," Aly said to her sister. "I think we should add Suzy Davis and Suzy's Spectacular Makeup to our booth. She can do all the makeup, and we'll make more money for the girls' side. Hopefully, we'll win and get to go to the water park."

"*Suzy Davis?*" Brooke said, tugging on her braid. "But we spend all our time trying to get *rid* of Suzy Davis!"

"I know, I know," Aly replied. "But Suzy's Spectacular Makeup actually *is* a good idea. People really liked it on Picture Day, remember? Plus, even if she makes one dollar, that's one more dollar for the girls' team we didn't have before."

Brooke ran the end of her braid back and forth across her cheek. After a few seconds, she said,

"Okay, you're right. It'll help us win the water park. So I vote yes."

Aly hugged her sister and then went and told Charlotte and Lily the plan. She knew Brooke would tell Sophie.

Aly ran from Roll a Hole in One to Paint Your Face, from Balloon Darts to Soccer Score. No Suzy. For a minute she was afraid Suzy had already left the carnival, but she finally found her leaning against a tree, eating popcorn.

"Hey, Suzy," Aly said.

"Aren't you supposed to be at your Sparkle Spectacle booth, or whatever you called it?" Suzy answered, popping a kernel into her mouth.

"I am," Aly said, "but I . . . uh . . . I have an idea that I think you can help me with."

Suzy crunched the popcorn. "Why would I want to help you?" she asked.

Aly let out a huff of breath. "Because Charlotte and Lily and I helped you on School Picture Day. And because you want the girls to win and go to Water World."

Suzy stood up a little straighter. "I'm listening," she said.

Aly swallowed. She needed to convince Suzy, fast. "Remember how Principal Rogers told us we couldn't have the Sparkle photo booth?"

"Yes, because Aubrey's was better," Suzy said.

"Right," Aly said. "It was. But anyway, she said we were allowed to add a third thing for our booth. When I saw you walking by, I remembered how popular your makeup was on School Picture Day, and I thought maybe *you* could be our third thing. If you want to add Suzy's Spectacular Makeup to our booth, I think we could beat the boys."

Suzy ate another piece of popcorn. "Let's say I

wanted to do this," she answered. "I don't have my supplies here."

Aly thought for second. "Maybe you could pick them up from home. I saw your dad before. He could drive you home. Or your mom could bring your supplies here."

"My mom's working today," Suzy said.

"But your dad?" Aly was really hoping Suzy was going to say yes soon. There wasn't any time to waste.

"Okay. I guess I could ask my dad," Suzy finally said. "And just so you know, I'm only doing this because I love water parks."

"Of course," Aly said. She headed over to Principal Rogers to tell her their plan. On the way, she passed the boys' Tattoo You booth. A long line with everyone from first-grade girls to sixth-grade boys was wrapped around the booth. *Oh, boy,* Aly thought, *we've really got work to do.*

She hurried back to the Sparkle Spa Celebration booth, filled in the girls about Suzy, and returned to braiding and polishing.

A little while later, AP Amari came out with his bullhorn again.

"New numbers to report! The boys are now at five hundred seventy-eight dollars and the girls at five hundred twenty-one!"

Aly was not happy with this latest tally. Would her Suzy Davis plan turn things around? Where *was* Suzy, any—

"We're here!" Suzy suddenly appeared out of nowhere with her sister behind her. "Heather's going to help too," she announced. "Since you have two braiders and two polishers, it makes sense to have two makeup-ers. We'll set up over there." She pointed toward a corner of the booth next to the manicure stations, where a little bit of counter space was available.

"Great," Aly said.

Brooke rolled her eyes but agreed.

As soon as Suzy set up, she asked to borrow Sophie's chair. She stood up on it and started to yell, even louder than AP Amari with his bullhorn. "Attention! Attention! The Sparkle Spa Celebration now includes Suzy's Spectacular Makeup! If you want fairy dust or shimmer lip gloss, it costs one dollar! I would've had perfume, too, if Principal Rogers let me do my own booth. But now it's just fairy dust and lip gloss, so you can blame her."

Aly had to bite her bottom lip to keep from laughing at that last bit.

Before Suzy could even jump off the chair, girls came running. Suzy and Heather started applying makeup—well, Suzy did and yelled at Heather for not doing it right. Aly and Charlotte continued braiding, and Brooke and Sophie kept on manicuring.

The afternoon flew by, and before the girls knew it, it was time for Lily to hand money over to Principal Rogers again, and for Mr. Amari to read the results. "This is going to be a close race!" he said. "The boys have earned seven hundred ninety-nine dollars and the girls seven hundred fifty-five. The girls are closing the gap!"

"Just forty-four dollars from a tie. I think it's because of my makeup," Suzy said.

Brooke rolled her eyes again, but Aly smiled. She didn't care why the girls won, she just wanted them to win. She was still worried about the cookie bet and getting into trouble with her mom and Joan. If Suzy Davis was the reason the girls raised the most money, that was fine by her! She just hoped they could keep it up.

eight
Tie-Dye Tango

Two hours later, broken hair elastics lay on the ground, cotton balls overflowed the trash, and Suzy Davis had a thick smear of fairy dust on her white T-shirt. It looked a little like Tie-Dye Tango, a polish Mom had ordered last week.

The girls had been inching closer to the boys with each measurement, and last time Aly had checked the giant thermometer, the girls were at $1,744 and the boys at $1,756.

"Twelve dollars!" Lily kept saying. "They're only beating us by twelve dollars!"

Throughout the day, even though the Sparkle Spa booth was super busy, the girls had taken short breaks so that they could go to the carnival themselves—on the girls' side. They had gotten married to each other and decorated more cookies and played the Wheel of Fortune and took pictures at the Be a Super-Model booth, which Aly had to admit *was* a better photo booth than the one she and the girls would have made.

"Can we play balloon darts?" Brooke had asked right after she and Aly had taken pictures together wearing green alien headbands and blue boas.

Aly checked her pocket. "We've spent all our money!" she giggled.

Walking around the field, the girls saw lots of kids—and even some grown-ups—with tattoos, mainly the glow-in-the-dark ones, which they kept cupping their hands around their arms to see. The other boy booths were pretty busy too, especially Win a Fish.

"Do you think the girls are going to win?" Sophie asked when Aly and Brooke returned. She had just finished a Cotton Candyland polish job on Keisha, a second grader, and now Keisha was getting her makeup done.

"It's possible," Lily said, trying to count the wad of money in her hand. Every time she got halfway through, someone would hand her more money, and she would get mixed up and have to start counting all over again.

"Fifteen minutes until the end of the carnival!" boomed Mr. Amari.

Suzy Davis pushed Sophie off her chair and climbed up on it. "If you haven't gotten your makeup done yet, come now!" she yelled. "And get braided, too!"

Aly was impressed that Suzy remembered to talk about the braiding.

"What about manicures?" Brooke reminded her.

"And manicures, too!" Suzy shouted.

Brooke seemed satisfied, especially when a third grader came over and asked for purple fingernails, and then Daisy's little sister, Violet, requested blue ones. Aly flexed her fingers when Maisie came to the braid side of the booth and asked for three braids braided together. Aly got to work.

At 3:30 on the dot, AP Arami informed everyone that the carnival booths were closed. "Please deliver your last round of money to me and Principal Rogers and clean up your areas."

Charlotte held out a giant bag as one by one the girls threw out the day's garbage. Heather Davis was very happy with herself. "I did so much makeup today," she said. "Does that mean I get to be part of your business forever, Suzy?"

"I'll think about it," Suzy told her sister.

Aly turned to Brooke and gave her a Secret Sister Eye Message: *I'm glad we're Sparkle Spa partners.*

Brooke smiled and started packing polishes into the wheelie suitcase they had brought them in.

"I wonder what's taking so long," Lily said, checking her watch. "It shouldn't take this long to count the money."

"Maybe they want to be extra sure," Charlotte said. "There *is* a day at Water World on the line here."

And a batch of Joan's cookies, Aly thought.

Sophie nodded as she tied up a trash bag. "They do need to be sure."

Brooke had just finished rolling up the Sparkle Spa Celebration sign when AP Amari blew his whistle into the bullhorn. The shrill sound was deafening.

"I'm sorry it's taken us so long," he said, "but Principal Rogers and I counted, and counted again, and then recounted *all* of the money for each team.

We now have the official totals. The girls have made one thousand, nine hundred ninety-six dollars—"

Lily whooped. Aly and Charlotte cheered. And Sophie and Brooke jumped up and down. Heather jumped with them.

"It's not worth cheering until we hear how much the boys made," Suzy said, her arms crossed. Aly didn't like admitting it, but Suzy was right.

AP Amari continued. "And the boys have made one thousand, nine hundred ninety-seven dollars. Congratulations, boys, you won by one dollar!"

"One dollar!" Lily groaned.

Brooke looked like she was about to cry. "It's Dad's dollar," she said to Aly. "For the Sports Trivia. If he hadn't played Sports Trivia, they wouldn't have won."

Aly tried to think of something comforting to say, but Brooke was right. If Dad hadn't spent that dollar, the girls would've tied.

Charlotte looked dejected. Lily had collapsed onto a manicure chair. Sophie's head was in her hands. But Suzy Davis was crawling around on the ground.

"Suzy, *what* are you doing?" Aly asked.

Suzy looked up. "When Lily was counting money before, I thought I saw a dollar fall out of her hands. But then I wasn't sure, and I had to finish putting fairy dust on Keisha's cheeks. After that I didn't see it anymore. But maybe it got pushed to the side of the booth."

Aly got down on her hands and knees too. "And if a dollar really did fall . . . ," she started.

"Then we'd tie!" she and Suzy both said together.

"It's over," Lily said. "Besides, I don't think I dropped any money."

Even though Lily was upset, Charlotte had perked up. "Maybe Suzy did see you drop something. You never know, it might still be there."

Soon Charlotte was on the ground next to Aly. And then Brooke, Sophie, and Heather.

Then Heather gasped. "I found it!" she said. "I found it!" She tugged the corner of a dollar out from underneath one of the manicure chairs.

"Wait!" Suzy Davis yelled in her loudest voice, pulling her sister next to her. The Davis sisters ran over to Principal Rogers and AP Amari. Heather was gripping the dollar tightly in her hand. "We forgot a dollar! It was stuck to the bottom of a chair. The girls have one more dollar!"

Principal Rogers and AP Amari looked at each other.

"I'm not sure we can count this," Principal Rogers said. "It wasn't in by the deadline."

"But it was our dollar!" Suzy explained. "We made it fair and square. It just fell out of Lily's hands. Look, it even has fairy dust on it. That's how you know it's from our booth. Heather found it. Please let it count."

Aly and Brooke had followed Suzy and Heather. Aly was surprised at how reasonable and nice Suzy sounded.

"I'm not sure we can," Principal Rogers said again.

Just then a man with white hair and a white moustache walked over to Principal Rogers. He was wearing a sweatshirt that said WATER WORLD.

"Excuse me," he said, looking right at Suzy. He gestured to Principal Rogers and AP Amari to follow him. The three talked quietly. *Who is that?* wondered Aly.

"Thanks for sticking up for our booth," Aly said to Suzy while they waited.

Suzy shrugged. "Whatever," she said. "I just wanted to go to the water park."

Aly smiled. "Well," she said, "thank you anyway, no matter what your reason was."

A minute or so later, the white-haired man, AP Amari, and Principal Rogers walked back to the crowd that had formed around the Tanner and Davis girls. AP Amari spoke. "For those of you who don't know, this is Mr. Molina, the owner of Water World. We've just talked over the last-minute dollar with him, and Mr. Molina has said it will count."

At this, the girls on the field cheered and the boys booed.

"Which means," AP Amari said over the noise, "this competition ends in a tie. Mr. Molina will provide a free day at Water World for the entire school!"

Instead of booing this time, the boys cheered too.

Aly and Brooke looked at each other and started screaming as loudly as they could. Lily put two fingers in her mouth and whistled. And the Auden Angels broke out in their soccer cheer. "Go, Auden! Go, Angels! Go, Auden! Go, Angels!" they shouted.

"And what's more," AP Amari yelled, "Mr. Molina will be matching the three thousand, nine hundred ninety-four dollars we've raised for the Community Chest."

Everyone kept cheering.

"I'm so proud of all of you," Principal Rogers said, taking the bullhorn from AP Amari. "And I want everyone to thank Mr. Molina for everything he's done for us and for our community."

"Thank you, Mr. Molina!" everyone chorused.

"But really I think this happened because of you," Aly whispered to Suzy.

Suzy looked surprised. And then she surprised Aly by smiling at her. For the very first time since Aly had known Suzy Davis, she wondered if maybe there was a nice person underneath all Suzy's meanness. Just maybe.

nine

Light Bright

Not quite a week later, on Friday morning, Aly and Brooke were packing their backpacks for school. But instead of homework and lunches, it was bathing suits and towels and—at Mom's insistence—sunscreen.

"Are you girls ready?" Mom asked, jingling her car keys.

"So ready!" Brooke said, skipping out the door. "Sophie and I have a plan. First we're going to go down all the slides. Then the lazy river, and finally, the tide pool."

Aly smiled and slipped on her backpack. Brooke and Sophie had been talking about their plan all week—at school, at the Sparkle Spa, on the phone after dinner.

"Do you want to know the order of the slides?" Brooke asked as they all got into Mom's car. "Because we made an order." Brooke chattered the whole way to school, but Aly was thinking of one last thing she had to do before they went to Water World.

Aly and Charlotte met at the front doors of Auden. Aly opened her backpack and took out a container of cookies. *Joan's cookies.*

Even though the carnival had ended in a tie, the girls still felt they owed Cameron his winnings. Right after the carnival, Aly and Charlotte had confessed their problem to Mom and Joan. Mom wasn't pleased, but Joan said as long as Aly and Charlotte helped her bake the cookies, she didn't mind. Brooke helped too, even though she was a little mad Aly hadn't told her about it either.

The girls walked over to the buses lined up for Water World. Charlotte spotted Cameron, standing in front of Caleb. She took the container from Aly and handed it to him.

"You won the bet, fair and square, Cameron. And I bet these are the best cookies you'll ever taste."

"Thanks, Charlotte," he answered. "That's really nice of you. I guess girls—well, at least you and Aly—are pretty cool."

Once they were at Water World, Aly, Charlotte, and Lily teamed up with Caleb, Garrett, and Cameron, and the six of them raced up Rocket Launcher for their fourth trip down. It was nice being friends with the boys again instead of enemies.

"Rocket Launcher is the best water slide in this whole place!" Caleb said, sliding his tube onto his shoulder so it would be easier to climb the ladder.

Lily slipped her tube over her head. "It totally is," she agreed.

Aly thought so too. When she was almost at the top of the ladder, she turned around to look out at the rest of the park and all of Auden Elementary sliding, swimming, and racing.

At the bottom of the ladder, Aly saw Suzy Davis, alone. Just like that, she made a decision.

"I'll meet you guys at the top," she said.

"Are you sure?" Charlotte asked.

Aly nodded and pointed toward Suzy Davis. "I just want to tell her something."

Aly stuck her arm through her tube, the way Caleb had done, and climbed back down the ladder.

"Hey, Suzy," she said. "Why don't you slide with

us today? The Rocket Launcher is really fun. And I told everyone else I'd meet them on top. So . . . if you want, you can come too. They're waiting up there."

"They're waiting for *you*," Suzy said, rolling her tube back and forth. "Not me."

"Same thing," Aly said. "Really, you should come."

Suzy took a deep breath. "Well, I guess one slide with you guys wouldn't kill me." She paused. "But don't think this means we're friends. I would never be friends with someone who wore a bathing suit with smiley faces."

Aly looked down at the smiley faces on her bathing suit. Suzy couldn't be serious, *could she*? Aly turned around and noticed there was a smile playing across Suzy's mouth.

"Oh, of course," Aly said. "I would never expect you to be friends with someone who liked smiley-face bathing suits."

Suzy bit her lip but then started laughing. Aly started laughing too.

Aly didn't know what she and Suzy Davis were, but they certainly weren't enemies anymore. And maybe that was the best thing to happen because of the carnival. Even better than a day at Water World.

How to Give Yourself (or a Friend!) a Bling It On Sparkle Pedicure

By Aly (and Brooke!)

✳ ⸱ ⸱ ✳ ⸱ ⸱ ⸱ ✳ ⸱ ⸱ ⸱ ✳ ⸱ ⸱ ⸱ ✳

What you need:

Paper towels

Polish remover

Cotton balls

(or more paper towels)

A bottle of clear polish

A bottle of super-bright, super-sparkly polish

(We think a bright sparkly red feels perfect for a carnival, but you can choose whichever color you want!)

What you do:

1. Put some paper towels on the floor—or wherever you're going to put your feet. (This is so you don't get sparkles on the carpet or floor-or grass or sidewalk if you're polishing outside. Which is a lovely place to polish, by the way.)

2. Take a cotton ball or a piece of paper towel and put some polish remover on it. If you have polish on your toes already, use enough to get it off. If you don't, just rub the remover over your nails once to get off any dirt that might be on there. (It might make lumps. Or show through if you chose a lighter color.) Also, for some reason this makes the nail polish stick better.

3. Rip off two more paper towels. Roll the first one into a tube and then twist it so it stays tube-shaped.

Then weave it back and forth between your toes to separate them a little bit more. After that, do the same thing with the second paper towel. You might need to tuck it in around your pinkie toe if it pops up and gets in your way while you polish—you can also cut it to make it shorter if you want. (Or just fold the tube before you start weaving, so it's the right size.)

4. Open up your clear polish and put a coat of clear on each nail. Then close the clear bottle up tight. (You can do your toes in any order, but Aly usually starts with my big toes and works her way to my pinkies.)

5. Open up the bright, sparkly polish. Put a coat on each toe. (If you're in a rush, you can skip to step seven. But we like to do a second coat

to make the color extra bright and extra sparkly.)

6. Repeat step five. Then let the polish dry for about two minutes. (Basically, if you sing "Happy Birthday" to yourself twice through, that'll be long enough. Or you can sing "Happy Birthday" to someone else.)

7. Open up your clear polish. Put a top coat of clear polish on all of your toes. Close the bottle up tight.

8. Now your toes have to dry for about twenty minutes (though it could take longer). You can fan them for a long time, or sit and make a bracelet or read a book or watch TV or talk to your friend (or sister!) until you're all dry. (One way to test is to very carefully touch your big toe with the

pad of your thumb. If it's not at all sticky, you're probably done.)

And now you should have a sparkly Bling It On pedicure! Even after the polish is dry, you probably shouldn't wear socks and closed-up shoes for a while. Bare feet or sandals are better so all your hard work doesn't get smooshed. (And so you can show off your fancy feet!)

Happy polishing!

✳ ⸱ ⸱ ✳ ⸱ ⸱ ✳ ⸱ ⸱ ✳ ⸱ ⸱ ✳

Did you LOVE reading this book?

Visit the Whyville...

Where you can:

○ Discover great books!

○ Meet new friends!

○ Read exclusive sneak peeks and more!

Log on to visit now!
bookhive.whyville.net